Dedication

Lord, I dedicate this book back to you firstly. There was a long journey that I went on (a whole year) to get this project out for you. Some days I was lazy, some days I was scared, some days, I was just plain disobedient. However, I thank you for your Grace in helping me get through this. Always letting me know, reminding me that you were proud of me, and always putting the fire under me when needed. Thank you for seeing my potential but also writing my story and knowing exactly what's inside of me. You helped me to understand that I possess the power to get it done and for that I thank you. Please continue to bring me and every person reading this book guidance in their lives. I thank you so much !

I would also like to Dedicate this book to my Husband and Son! You all pushed me like no other! Keane Muirhead, you are the love of my life, my back bone, my helper, my biggest supporter and I love you! You listened to me read this whole book through and through in one day and I knew then you would be such a special part in this process. Thank you for your love but most of all your support. Thank you also for giving me my son. If only I had known he would drive me to finish all of my goals so quickly! Kingston Muirhead, know that you are a driving force in mommy's happiness and you and daddy mean the world to mommy! To my boys, I love you forever and always.

Chapter 1: Woe is Me

As I walked into the unassuming office and sat on the hard chair waiting for my name to be called amongst about 30 other people, I sat in awe of how many people were in my same predicament. However, I still felt my situation was so much worse. As I scanned over the faces in the room, not even one of them looked nearly as young as I did. Immediately, I wanted to jet out of the door as I noticed the older women scrunching their eyebrows at me. I knew they wanted to ask in the loving but nosey way only us women can do, "why are you here, baby?" But I sat down and let my mind wander.

I wonder, how is it that I'm here?!? I did everything right. I prayed. I went to church regularly, I tried to keep my goodies to myself, I was respectful, kind, and faithful to my boyfriend (let's call him Jay), maybe too faithful. I led by example with my finances and was very frugal. I worked two jobs, and I was a hard worker. *How did I get here?* And how is it that the people who caused this, get to run scot-free?

As I sat down, I zoned out thinking of how my parents never taught me the importance of finances. I thought about how Jay is roaming scot-free even though he had a huge part to play in this predicament. I couldn't ignore the, "my people have been systematically oppressed for years" argument. Every person, place, or thing I was blaming. At this point I'm deep in my blame rant when I hear my name called.

"Ms. Davilia Beckwith!"

My name never sounded so loud, clear, sharp, and scary all at the same time. I got that feeling you get when your mom calls your name because she's about to pass out a butt whooping she owed you from something you did earlier. Just like back then, tears streamed down my face almost immediately from hearing my name called. Nonetheless, I got up from my seat, held back as many tears as I could and followed the figure down the hall. I really couldn't make the person out because they were turned around but mostly because of the tears swelling up in my eyes. It was my turn to face my truth. Also, this meant it was my turn to let go of everything that had me bound in my life.

However, I was still too angry to let it go. Holding on to that anger became my safe place. After all, I had a right! I felt I had been robbed and the main thief was still on the loose to go on to his next victim! Actually, forget that last part, I wasn't even worried about the other victims if I'm being honest. Just, how could he do this to me? My rightful selfishness in this moment took captive of any empathy I could feel for others. I was worried about myself....

As I waited for the lawyer to enter the office, I thought about my early childhood. Incredibly early in my life, I learned or was taught that other people's happiness was more important than my own. And not intentionally in the depressing sort of way. It crept in and happened very slowly and quietly. Kind of like the anaconda before it swallows its prey, you almost never know where it came from but by the time it's there, it's too late. I guess it came from having to look out for my little brother while my mom was always working, maybe from the lack of acknowledgment from my father, or maybe it came from not valuing myself because I never really knew what value was or even experienced it first-hand. Either way, it didn't matter at this point, I was in too deep. So here I am, with all these thoughts running through my head as I'm filing for bankruptcy at 22 years young.

Finally, the lawyer came in a little behind me and I sat there waiting for her to close the door and take her seat across the long desk in front of me. We made small talk until she sat down, which made me think how I *really hate* small talk because it just reminds me of another meaningless thing in my life. In my opinion, people make small talk because they hate silence. As I'm going on yet another rant in my head, she interrupts me by saying, "Is this the list of everything you owe?" In my head I'm thinking, *you mean everything that he owes?*

"Yes ma'am," I answered.

"Please go through your list of debts to make sure everything is there," she says.

As I'm going through the list, I couldn't fathom how much debt I had accumulated during this short time of life.

I always said I would never be the one to do this. To follow in the same footsteps of my family before me with poor financial habits. But, for the right person or situation you can find yourself going against yourself very quickly. Anyway, as I'm thumbing through the pages of accumulated debt, I'm thinking to myself again, *How did I get here?* Almost on queue the lawyer asks the same question, as if my thoughts were appearing on a teleprompter.

I looked up to answer her and this was the first time I actually got a good look at her and realized I couldn't give some lame excuse about the systematic oppression of my people because she looked just like me. Black, long hair, glasses, the whole 9. At that point, I was extremely nervous because this would be the first time, I told my story to a stranger.

"How did I get here?" I said aloud repeating her and myself.

"Well, it started the day I went to the Nissan dealership and purchased a car. I asked Jay, my then boyfriend, to come along. But let me be clear, he did not have any financial ties to my car. I simply needed a new car because the old one was dying on me. And at this point I know you are like, so what was the point of having him there in the first place, right? Well, at the time, I was not comfortable with doing anything with adults by myself. I was about 20 or 21-years-old..."

The lawyer interjected, "So, Ms. Beckwith, how does purchasing yourself a car end you up in my office?"

I couldn't tell if she was growing impatient with me or if she was genuinely engaged and wanting to hear the next part of the story. I continued anyway, I knew I had to go into my insecurities, and I couldn't tell the story without going into the relationship that got me here.

Chapter 2: Insecurities

"I had serious insecurities of Jay leaving me, me not contributing enough in our relationship, and honestly me not living up to his mother. Jay was a huge mama's boy and a family man. I tried my best to do what women do in relationships all too often though. I tried to change him. Now that we got that out the way, let's go back to the dealership. So, I finished getting my new car and it was amazing. However, after Jay was at the dealership supporting me, a couple days later *he* wanted a new car. Although, his current car was just fine from my knowledge, but because of his credit being horrible, he was unable to get one on his own. Me, being the gullible person I was at the..."

"Ms. Beckwith don't tell me you got that man a car?!?" The lawyer interjected.

"I guess you could see where I was going with this." I responded after hearing her disappointment.

"However, technically two days later, I turned around and financed myself another car in my name and gave it to him. He was fine with me purchasing the car for him after I almost kind of pressured him into it. I felt like at this point he could give his old car to his family and they wouldn't need him around as much anymore. You see, back then he would have to take various family members back and forth to work and do odd jobs around his mom's house. BUT I was trying to get him to spend more time with me. I wanted him to see that I was truly *down* for him and only him, and that I was worth committing to.

I really wanted to get married back then. "So, I purchased him the car to, frankly, get him off his mama's hip. Not knowing that if he didn't want to go, he wouldn't."

At this point, tears started to swell in my eyes as if they were sponges. The Lawyer tried to comfort me.

"Hunny, this wasn't your first mistake made about a man and I can guarantee you, it won't be the last."

Her comment wasn't comforting at all. It's like when people say, "Sorry for your loss," when someone dies or "great" when asked how their day is going. Just ritualistic and non-helpful.

"So, what happened next?" she asked.

"Well, after getting him the car, I was so happy. But the General Manager and other sales reps in the dealership tried to make us understand the gravity of what I was doing/ just did. Some of the managers of the dealership even tried to have a separate talk with Jay to let them know how awesome of a girlfriend I was. They also asked him what seemed like a thousand times if he were going to marry me or when we would get married. Everyone was so persistent that I believe if the dealership could've married us right then, they would've built a chapel on the edge of the mechanic shop out back and hired an officiant. None of that stopped me though because that day Jay still left with a new car and he and I went around to his family's house and everyone was so excited. Some said, "Oh they both got new cars." My ego allowed me to feel on top of the world after hearing them brag about how nice the cars were. But that soon came crashing down."

I paused because I needed a moment, but I continued.

"About a month later, I got the urge to really tell someone what I had done. So, I called up my godmother, Linda. She immediately told me I should not have done that, and I made a big mistake. However, now that it is done, I need to get him to sign a promissory notice. So, I drafted one up within the following week or two. I sent the notice to him and he said to me, "If you did this out of the kindness of your heart (referring to the car) for me why would you give me this document and I don't feel comfortable going into a legal agreement with you." At this point, he offered for me to take the car back and bring it back to the dealership. What was I going to do? The time for me to be able to take that car back would've long expired by that time and because the car was a 2013 model and I got it in 2017 I'm sure the dealership was very excited when we took that car off of their hands and would not return. And to be completely honest, I would've been extremely embarrassed taking the car back!"

"So, what did you do?" The lawyer asked.

"I did what any insecure woman would do. I told him, "no baby I trust you. I don't think you would do anything to hurt me." I allowed **codependency** and my own vain desires to make the decision for me. Part of me was also very nervous about taking the car back because I didn't know what else to do. I felt as if I told him I was taking the car back he wouldn't have trusted me to do anything for him going forward. He told me several times that his own family hadn't done anything like this for him, so what was I to do? I let my ego win that battle."

At this point I paused for a moment from telling my past and I started to wander off in my own mind again while she was keying on her computer. I thought about those lessons learned. I learned that insecurities are my biggest enemy. People spend money they don't have on clothes and in my case, cars they don't need, to fill a void they themselves can't fill. No matter how much money or time they invest in their own physical reconstruction, or in my case, attaining materials, they're still unhappy with who they see in the mirror. All of us change things about ourselves, of course. But, changing your appearance on the outside with clothes, cars, and jewelry will only help how other people see you. I realized that at the end of the day, I still had to come home to myself. When he rejected me, after all that I did for him, I hated myself more...

"Ms. Beckwith.... Is everything okay?" She asked as she brought me back to reality from my own thoughts.

"Yes ma'am, just needed a moment," I answered.

"So, can you explain all of these insurance charges?" She asked as she handed me another list of companies I owed.

"Well, I had insurance with Jay, and I allowed him to cover all of the bills. So, it was his job to find us good insurance. I didn't realize he was not paying the insurance for a couple months and leaving outstanding balances. I later found out he was hopping around from vendor to vendor. Our insurance was already high because of his traffic violations and I think he was involved in an accident as well. So, we were paying extremely high insurance. Stack that on top of the fact that we were both under 25 and that's the fastest way we consistently lost $1,000 a month. I was empty. Actually I was more than empty because empty implies that I was at zero. No, I was at a negative balance. I mean that literally, you'll see! "

My lawyer stated, "The car situation, although tragic, it still doesn't give me everything on how you got here? Oh, by the way, can you sign this?" As she passed me a document.

I let out a big sigh because signing on the dotted line was something all too familiar to me.

"We can wait until the end if you'd like?" She proposed.

I guess she saw the look of trauma and hesitation on my face. I proceeded to tell the story and waited to sign.

"Well, next came all of my credit cards. I added him as an authorized user on all of my accounts and ordered him his own cards so that he would feel like the MAN when purchasing things for the house and himself."

"And he maxed them out?" The lawyer asked.

"Yes!" I responded. "But not on his own. To be honest I feel I had my share in it too."

"How so?" She asked.

"Well, I applied for a huge credit card that I got approved for. I was going to use it to pay off my student loans because I would have a better interest rate and only need to pay one person. At the time it made sense, don't ask."

Never attempt to pay off debt with debt!

"Although, it was a silly idea it was better than what I actually did with the card."

"What'd you do with the card Ms. Beckwith?" The lawyer asked.

"I allowed my insecurity of **not fitting in** to rule my decision. I took his family on vacation, about 6 people including myself. We were on vacation for about a week or so. I was still doing all these things for his family to love me and to gain more love from him because part of me always felt like if I wasn't giving then he wasn't loving. But I hushed that voice and chucked it up as negativity trying to come between me and my future. After all, I was still holding on to the idea of us being married with babies someday. I always felt like I didn't quite fit in with his family, so while I did this because it would put a smile on their face. I mainly just wanted them to truly love me. I wanted them to accept me and believe I was a great person and ultimately a great girlfriend to Jay. So, I kept going on with the lie I constantly told myself."

"And what was that?" she asked.

"That I was enough for him; that I was the love of his life; and that we were going to get married someday. You name it, my mind fantasized and romanticized it up! I had been in Lala land and living in the clouds while he was on earth with clear vision and trying to move further and further away. I continuously allowed myself to think that he was **the one for me**. I figured he would one day magically have some revelation about how amazing I was and see my value."

How did I think that he would see how amazing I was or my value, when I didn't see it? I was still scared of losing him.

Chapter 3: My Codependency

Codependency is described as an excessive emotional or psychological reliance on a partner, typically one who requires support on account of an illness or addiction. You see, I had literally psyched myself into thinking I needed him. Have you ever been in a haunted house or an escape room by yourself or even with a group and realized when something popped out at you; you grabbed ahold of someone or something you had no intention of pulling close to you? That's what fear does to you. Fear causes you to jump suddenly and grab ahold to someone you had no intention of being that close to.

I told the lawyer, "I feared the unknown. So, I gravitated to what was familiar. I feared what life would be like without him and if I would struggle without him."

I had this fear, not realizing in the moment that I was struggling more with him than when I was by myself.

The lawyer was listening intently as I continued, "I feared separation, embarrassment, and to be perfectly honest that the hard work I put in, someone else would come right along and reap the benefits! Or for that matter, that he would leave me period and go frolicking in the horizon with his new life at my expense! These were all valid for me because I genuinely loved him. However, I can honestly say I feared opposition as well. I let my guard all the way down and stopped fighting for myself. Because of that fear, I continued to just play it safe and stay. If someone came along and gave me the slightest nudge on my shoulder, it would have probably left a bruise. I was so fragile back then. I had forgotten how to fight for the right things. The things that actually mattered in this world. Actually, the things that mattered to me!"

"Ms. Beckwith, do you need a moment?" She asked hearing my voice go out.

"No!" I responded and continued. "Codependency and countless other insecurities mixed with a little depression caused me to stop working out, to stop eating healthy, to stop doing basic things like taking care of my own hair and washing my face. I remember during the week he would only come home to eat, take a shower, watch some TV, and go to bed. Most nights he'd be at his mom's until late. It started out as just on the weekends then he incorporated some Thursdays into this trend too. Then it got to the point where it seemed he was just utterly annoyed by my presence. This just played on my insecurity of **not being good enough.** He constantly made me feel like there was always something else he'd rather be doing. I would call him and sometimes he wouldn't answer and sometimes when he did, he would just play like he was asleep so that he could use the excuse, "I'm too tired to drive home." Or he'd fall asleep over his mom's home and wouldn't come home to me.

"During this time in my life you could've called me something like a Stepford wife. I cooked and cleaned and washed everything; smiled and grinned except I wasn't handing my man a pen so he could write that check, paying all my bills as the Tyler Perry Play would say. At this time, I can honestly say is when I was sucked into believing this was the kind of life I was supposed to live. I just had to put in the hard work and dedication. Or as Ms. Betty Wright would say, "No pain, no gain!" So, I stuck it out."

"And you thought this was healthy?" She questioned, without really looking for an answer.

I looked at her and continued my story. "I was doing so many "wifey" things for this man. Ironing clothes, cooking dinner, packing lunches, picking out his outfits, setting out his clothes for him to shower. Just small things, that I hoped he noticed, not because he asked me to but because I genuinely wanted him to be happy."

Reading that back, I had a child not a boyfriend. For ladies reading this, please don't do "wifey" things at the girlfriend price. Meaning don't invest so much into anything with little to no return on your investment. The goal is commitment and to be with someone that loves and values you!

But anyway, "I tried my best to keep the house clean and make things fun. I wanted him to spend more time at home with me. However, my efforts were not acknowledged with the response I was hoping for. After a while, even his family could tell I wasn't happy anymore. I went from the girl that was willing to wash dishes, get up and cook, and do everything to feeling used and abused."

"At least you started to see a pattern," she interrupted. "But please continue."

"Later on, Jay got a second job to help our household make ends meet. At this time, I thought he really cared about our home and was truly trying. Need I remind you, that he was a manager at a local call center, and I was a lead. We had plenty of money for a one-bedroom apartment but where was it all going?!? He never let me in on his finances, so I just left it alone. But you can always tell when things aren't right. No matter how many budget plans I made, there was never anything left over. In fact, my account was going negative EVERY pay period!

"I couldn't understand for the life of me where all the money was going. I didn't know how much he made exactly but I could only guess rough estimates. But I knew for sure it was more than $2000 a month because that's what I was making, and he was 2 positions above me and had picked up a second job. Our rent was only $895 a month at the time, so I really couldn't figure out where it was all going. But then it hit me..."

"What.... What? Don't leave me in suspense," the lawyer begged,

"Well, while my account was going negative and I was paying all that I could. This man was gambling it all away. He and his family would take day trips down to their favorite gambling spot at least once a month and hit local gas stations for their slot machines from time to time. When I realized what was going on I kind of got that feeling that you get when you're doing dishes, but people just continue to pile dishes in the sink adding to the load. I was worn out and irritated."

"I know that feeling all too well Ms. Beckwith," she said while shaking her head.

"I was irritated about the whole situation. Let's say I take out the fact that he was spending bill money to go down there. I was also upset because he knew I never wanted to go but never offered to plan sweet things for us on the weekends except once. It was one night we decided to get dinner and a movie and all we did was constantly bicker back and forth. The relationship had gotten so boring. However, I was still acting as if everything was okay. Deep in my mind I knew the vision of us that I painted, was now one stroke away from going off canvas. Still I continued to fight....

"Fighting became the only thing I knew how to do. But soon, that took its toll on me too. If I'm being perfectly honest, my skin was terrible, my hair was damaged, I didn't want to go to work or finish my schoolwork. The only thing I had energy for was this energy sucking relationship that I so desperately attempted to keep afloat. I threw a couple jabs, hooks, and even tried some uppercuts. But in the 12th round, I was left bleeding and knocked out in the middle of the ring. Mostly, from the scars I had given myself by holding on to the bottom rope of our relationship. I was in the ring, fighting alone. I eventually got to a point where I was tired of being tired, looking tired, and acting tired. I had to face reality."

Chapter 4: Reality

Reality was calling for me and I tried to run. Reality is described as the word or the state of things as they actually exist, as opposed to an idealistic notional idea of them. Do you ever have preconceived notions about how things could be?

"So, did you communicate that this behavior bothered you?" The lawyer asked.

"Well, yes and no. I did tell him it bothered me that he wouldn't come home, to the point where it constantly felt like nagging to him. However, I didn't communicate everything to him, like why I wanted him around, or how it actually played on my childhood insecurities of **rejection and abandonment.**"

"Why not communicate these insecurities, especially based on how you lost the energy to take care of yourself?" She asked.

"I was too insecure and afraid of **saying how I truly felt**. I thought he'd leave me for good. After all, he wasn't responsible for repairing the damage or bandaging the wounds that were in my world long before him. After a while though, emptiness was the only thing I knew."

There are a couple definitions that dictionary.com describes as emptiness and I found that during that time of my life I was every one of them.

1. Emptiness - The state of containing nothing
2. Emptiness - The quality of lacking meaning
3. Emptiness - The quality of having no value or purpose

My lawyer looked at me and asked, "So, Ms. Beckwith what about your support system? I hate to ask but did you try alternatives before seeking my services?"

"I thought turning to anyone for help was out of the question. As far as my support system goes, during this period of my life, my romantic relationship wasn't the only thing that seemed as if it was failing. My career was stagnant, my relationship with my family was basically nonexistent, and my lack of accomplishments in school was enough to make me feel depressed within itself, without the added pressure of Jay. These things were like a domino effect in my life, as soon as one came falling down, here came another one like clockwork. I completely gave up on life and started allowing things to just … happen."

A lot of times in life we can just allow life to start happening to us instead of picking up the pieces and being accountable for the role we had to play in why our lives are the way they are.

I continued, "Now, don't get me wrong, there are some things in life that just … happen. Whether we caused them or not. However, we are focused on what we can control right now. My mom would say life is 10% what happens and 90% how you respond to it. Speaking of her, my mom and I weren't speaking at the time either.

"You see, at the time I didn't trust my mom with communicating with me, with helping me grow into a woman, or with finances. All due to the habits she showed me during my development years. In my opinion, what was she going to do for me in this situation? Nothing. In fact, she had just completed filing bankruptcy herself. Going to my godmother, Linda, was out of the question because I was too ashamed to go to her after the car situation. However, there was one person I knew I could talk to, but because of my relationship and not allowing others to influence my decisions, I also stopped talking her. One of the people I admired the most, my other god-mom, Naimah."

After I told this to the lawyer, she began keying vigorously on her keyboard. I started to feel like a case study. I kind of liked when she did though because it left me to my thoughts.... It sucks that retrospect is always 20/20.

"You ever go through something and stop talking to the one person you need to talk to the most? Over the years, Naimah became that person in my life. You know? The one that would call you out when you were wrong, but still did it in a loving way and didn't hold it against you after you made the wrong decision even after they advised against it? Yea, she loved me through my mess, and I shut her out for fear of being called stupid, honestly. As well as fear of my boyfriend's ego being bruised. Or I should say MY ego being bruised. She, along with other family members really did not like Jay, and at this point I truly understand why. But anyway, I sheltered myself and stayed away from my family out of fear that they would try to come between me and him. Also, I knew she would show me a mirror. And if I'm being honest, she would be able to call my bluff and see where I was truly hurting. There is nothing worse than someone seeing straight through to your soul and noticing, not glancing nor looking but taking notice of who you are when you are trying to hold it all together."

I stopped to think about all that I was holding together, and it came down to my soul. I lived my childhood managing my soul incorrectly, though I had no idea what a soul was. I later found that my soul was made up of characteristics that I had been taught to cover up: My mind, which was great when I used it like in school, maintaining a high GPA but not if I wanted to question things that didn't seem right. Next, my will, which was great unless I practiced free-will. Finally, my emotions, which showed I was alive and yea that's great unless I wanted to express it loudly or how I wanted.

This toxic behavior from my childhood translated so easily into my adulthood that I had no idea about it until just now, writing the previous paragraph. Isn't it crazy how things sneak up on you like that?! You go through life thinking that everything is normal - until some life altering experience like... I don't know, bankruptcy comes along to make you realize how much you really need Jesus! While going through this process you may even uncover new things about yourself. These experiences bring that out of you. However, the good thing is you gain a perspective on a lot of things. Such as, your personal standards and ideals of yourself. Delta Goodrem says, "Anyone who has gone through a life- changing experience will tell you there is a different understanding of what is real and what is important, and when you are going through different moments, you can reflect and go, 'I have been through worse." In other words, you will get through this and like the old saying goes, "What doesn't kill you makes you" - well you know the rest.

Back to me being petrified now. I was so nervous about talking to my God-mom about all of this. I was the most terrified that she would see right through my "I'm okay" façade and that all the bricks made of clay that I built the foundation of my relationship on would be washed away by the tears I would spill in just a single one-on-one talk with my god-mom. She had a way of making me pour out everything that was wrong. Whether I wanted to or not.

I felt like she knew that too. I knew she knew something was wrong with me. She'd ask, "where's your light?" It didn't go out but by this time it was very dim. My God mom has always told me I have a way of lighting up every room I walk into. I never knew it until I realized it was just about gone. She was talking about the glow that's evident that the Holy Spirit lives within. That glow that no one else can give. The kind of glow that comes when you have true peace and joy in your life. I had lost that because I had truly lost those qualities in my life.

I had no peace and didn't have true joy. And please don't mistake me, I'm not speaking about the day-to-day happiness that's ever-fleeting. Or the sense of satisfaction that one feels when you've been able to nab the parking space closest to the grocery store entryway, but true joy. I hadn't felt it in a while....

At the time, I was very much alone. I was trying to also deal with my daddy issues as well. But nothing too specific to talk about there, just another story of a woman growing up without her father.

As far as friends went, I didn't exactly have any. I was trying my best to make friends with Jay's sister and his brother's girlfriend, but they didn't seem to want to truly accept me in their circle at first. You remember the ones I took on vacation earlier? Right. Looking back on it though, I'm grateful for that. Not because they're bad people or anything but because I realize I never did fit in with them. You must realize that sometimes, rejection from others is a blessing, you don't belong to them anyway. This taught me that rejection doesn't mean I'm not good enough. Decide in your mind that you are the best thing that could've happened to someone's life since Spring water. Rejection just means the other person failed to notice what you have to offer. The way I see it, It's not your fault that they're blind. People normally reject expensive things because they can't afford them. You are a luxury item. Know your worth. Besides, authentic design will hardly ever go on sale ...

I understand it's all a process that will take some time though. I remember constantly wanting, no needing to feel validated. It was such a roller coaster. Because, while I went into the relationship physically fit, great credit, independent, working hard. I found myself becoming socially awkward, losing confidence by the milliseconds, poor credit, and gaining more weight than my ankles could hold. No seriously, my ankles couldn't hold the weight at all to this day I can still crack them!

I was out of money, out of available credit, out of people to run to, and out of numbers on the scale. To top it all off, I felt like I wasn't deserving of God's grace, mercy, or love so I really wasn't running to Him either.

Running to God started to feel like a punishment or a chore o bet honest. I started to get that feeling you got as a child when you know you've done something wrong but you *HAVE* to tell your parents because they'll find out anyway. I felt this way for so long because I knew I was also to blame, and I didn't want to hear from God too. I had ignored God for far too long. I truly believe because of that, ignoring my own intuition and not valuing my own opinion I was left in a state of overextend myself. Especially financially! I've learned that when I don't listen to the holy spirit, or the unction of my own voice, it will most times leave me in a worse than where I started. He did say obedience is better than sacrifice.

Have you ever said to yourself, "Dang, I knew that was going to happen? I should've gone with my first... instinct!" Instinct, gut, intuition, thought, whatever you said; yes, you're exactly right. Don't ignore those signs because in the end you'll be the one left empty.

"Ms. Beckwith?" My lawyer brought me back to reality.

"Yes ma'am?" I answered.

"Why do you want to include your checking account in this case?" She asked as she reviewed the packets again.

"Well, after a while, my account was consistently going negative while his was perfectly fine. I couldn't fathom how he thought this was okay. Jay explained it as, "It's the same money. Because your limit is $500 to go negative and you have $500 of your check left (after the bank took the $500 from the account being negative my previous pay period.) which gives you the same $1000." I tried my best to explain to him that, not only is that completely not how that works, but that even if this was true, the bank would eventually close my account for having a negative balance so many times. We all know once your account is negative it's very hard to come out of that cycle unless you have an additional source of income or miraculously became debt free. That way I could allocate that money specifically to catching the account back up. Seeing as neither of those happened for me, the account stayed in the negative. I also attempted to explain to him that there were charges every time the card was swiped, and the account was continuing in the negative. I knew he understood good and well, after all he was extremely smart, but I guess just like me, he was ignoring the facts."

"What do you mean by that?" She questioned.

Before I could gather my thoughts and answer....

Knock! Knock! The lawyer had her next session and it was time for me to go. I guess we were out of time, but she had already finalized everything. Turns out she just wanted to hear my story. I quickly put on my big girl panties and signed the documents that she wanted me to sign earlier as she motioned for me to leave her office and directed me out into the hallway. I was happy that part happened so quickly because had it not, I probably would've never signed those documents.

While walking down the hallway, I could feel the stares of those same women that were waiting in the lobby when I first arrived. However, this time I didn't have to wait for my name to be called to escape the awkward stares and dead silence of the room that was only interrupted by the sound of the next person's name being called or an occasional gum pop.

My lawyer motioned for me so I walked into the next room. She advised I would have to sit down at a computer and take a financial literacy competency test and speak with a virtual financial advisor.

"Excuse me, is this the last step?

"For now, yes. The hard part is over."

"Congratulations! You've made it through." I said to myself

As I was doing the test, I realized it was going to be hard for me because of the deep questions being asked. But I did it, since it was a requirement in the bankruptcy process. While sitting there, I felt that same sense of entitlement trying to creep in. I was in my head like, "I know all of this." I'm sure my slouched posture in the uncomfortable chair and boughetto (bougie and ghetto) countenance depicted that very well. I quickly brought myself back to reality and humbled myself enough to be real with myself and say, "If you truly knew this, you wouldn't be here girl."

In that moment I freed myself and gave myself grace. Recognizing that I was part of the problem freed me from the concerned of the stares of people around me. It's not liked they stopped starring, I just didn't care about them anymore.

The questions the financial literacy test presented made me think about how truly isolated I had made myself over time. The virtual Financial advisor asked me questions such as if I had an accountability partner? I understood it as someone I trusted very much to not only be honest with me but who I could open up to and communicate openly and effectively with. For most adults, that person would have been their spouse, siblings, best friends, or parents. We obviously know spouse was out of the question for me, thus why you're reading this now. As far as siblings go, I'm the oldest so that rules out the munchkins, and I've never truly had a best friend in my adult life. So that just leaves my parents. Of course, we already established that my father wasn't in the picture, but my mom. My mom was there but I convinced myself that there was no way I could do this with her.

I continued with the financial literacy test and they asked me if I knew what a budget was and how to stick to one. This reminded me of the countless budgets Jay and I put together even though it was obvious nothing was working. Though I tried my hardest to stick to one, eventually dysfunction prevailed.

I continued the test and it was honestly very informative. It taught me about what my qualifications would look like for home ownership in the future. It also taught me that most car dealerships have a program specifically for people who have filed bankruptcy. So, if you've had to file bankruptcy before just know this isn't the end of the road. I found that creditors do still want to deal with you.

As I completed the test and printed out 2 copies of my results, one for myself, and one for the lawyer, I realized the life I knew once before had slipped away from me and I had become completely about him, his needs, and wants and so was he.

I was ignoring everything that made sense. I allowed myself to become so engrossed in another person's life, that I forgot my own and before I knew it, that familiar feeling of loneliness set in. For a split second, maybe out of habit or perhaps it was the loneliness but I thought of texting Jay. I quickly steered myself away from Stupid Road and thought, "What's good with having someone around that's not helping?!" Good thing I caught myself. Once I did, I came back to reality. I was finished with the competency test and I knew my life was about to change. I walked through the lobby, not paying attention to anyone, and started to walk out to my car to leave, that's when I knew I had to decisions to make.

Chapter 5: Decisions

Heading home, I had this feeling of disbelief saying to myself, "I can't believe I just did that." I also felt a sense of satisfaction, like a weight had been lifted off my shoulders. I felt this undeniable feeling that a new beginning was on the horizon. I just didn't know how this new beginning was going to be and how I was going to handle it. My quiet car ride home allowed me to think about what I had just done. In that moment, I felt the happiest I had felt in a very long time. Although, most would say I didn't have anything or anyone, so why should I be happy. I learned that happiness does not just come externally, like from people. Happiness comes from the choices we make, just like love or any choice, you must make them yourself (for yourself). A lot of times when something terrible happens to you... Well, maybe I should speak from experience, sorry. Personally, when things happened to me that weren't favorable, I often blamed everyone else. But looking at it now, those terrible situations were caused by a lot of poor decisions that seemed small at the time but lead up to the big catastrophic mistakes.

My poor decisions caused me to lose so much that I held dear to me, which ultimately landed me in a very uncomfortable position. I was somewhere between holding on and letting go, which led me to staying still. I was literally stuck in every sense of the word. You see, being stuck was a decision because I made "convenient" my norm.

You see, it was convenient to have that jay around because then I wouldn't have to talk to God about my troubles. It was convenient to have him in my bed because I was scared most night. It was convenient to be around him all the time because then I'm "#relationship goals." It was even convenient to be around his family because then I didn't have to cook. "Did I just say that?"

Of course, in the moment, I did all those things out of the kindness of my heart and I genuinely wanted to be around him and his family. However, looking back, I realize that wasn't the best that God had for me. Heck, that wasn't even the best I had for me!

So, for those that are facing bankruptcy, whether it be mentally, emotionally, financially, or physically, one of the biggest lessons I learned was not to hold on to the past.... "Don't even try to." You'll end up making the process more painful than it needs to be. Also, understand that you are trading (not losing) your old mentally, emotionally, financially, and/or physically unstable life for a new one with a fresh new slate. No matter how many times you've filed bankruptcy. Be it, your first or fifth. You've got this!

Did you know the average millionaire files bankruptcy almost four times in their lifetime? So just know it can happen to anyone of us. No matter social status, race, ethnic background, or family lineage. The important part is to not stay down. You need to understand that you are not your mistakes and you are most certainly not your possessions. Separate yourself from the bankruptcy.

And I know.... I know. How can you do that when you're the main character in the story? I get it. Understand this, in God you are a new creation every single day. All that means is every day God gives you a new opportunity to be the best you. Every day you get a chance to make (or get) things right. Take it from me, try to choose sooner rather than later though. During my drive home I began thinking about how my life was about to change forever, I just smiled because I knew it would be for the better. But something happened. I got a call from a mutual friend of Jay and me and it literally set me back for a moment. It set me back in the sense that my mental growth in this situation had taken a few steps back.

In your journey, beware of these situations and people. These situations will leave you feeling like the wound is still fresh when you've already began the healing process. But of course, hindsight like retrospect is always 20/20 right?!

So, I had the conversation. During the conversation with this mutual friend, I started going on "how wrong Jay did me" and how I was literally just "leaving the law office to file bankruptcy." She could not believe everything that happened and was in complete disbelief. Looking back at it, so was I! I couldn't believe I allowed myself to get so vulnerable to the point where I spilled all of that to a mutual acquaintance. I felt so stupid.... Again. But I recovered and after the conversation was over, I told myself I wasn't going to mention anything else bad about him to others. Even if it's true. Thank God I didn't because later I learned that your words have power and consequences, so you need to speak what you want to see.

I was driving down 75 South and noticed a billboard that said, "Peaceful Sleep" with a mattress on it. I flashed back to how I would get out of bed and open up my blinds and talk to God and cry, feeling as though only the moon and God knew about those nights. So, I found myself crying next to a man at night who heard my cries but never turned to even wipe my tears. But even then, I tried to stifle my cries, careful not to wake him. I was so use to stifling my emotions that I kept everything bottled up and kept a bottle beside me. No seriously, I kept a bottle of Hennessy either next to or under my bed and would drink it every night. Within two nights I would finish one bottle. Sad, I know.

My decisions made me question and hate myself. "How could I be so stupid?" Scratch that. "How could I be so insane?" The definition of insanity is literally doing the same thing and expecting a different result. So, if you're reading this and thinking about going back to him/her or that toxic situation. This is your sign.... DON'T!

Down the line, I realized that the decisions I made were not only selfish because they impacted me but they impacted my relationships and work environment. I continued to drive though....

At this point, I thought I had to crawl back into God's good graces. Turns out, He was already welcoming me with open arms. He was watching me the entire time and was calling for me. I just was ignoring the signs and His voice because of my insecurities and my codependency. God never wanted to see me go through anything that I did. He wanted to love me, He wanted to hold me, HE wanted to hear how everything hurt me. I constantly wanted to run away. I realized I was doing the same thing to God that I was doing with my family... Shutting Him out. I remember thinking, "not anymore" as I broke the silence in my car by listening to gospel singer, Tasha Cobbs.

My world felt dark and not very fulfilling, but I was coming out. Have you ever put everyone before you? Your health? Your finances?

I've allowed that to happen to me too. It's completely not okay to always put everyone and everything else before you and your needs. Take a moment to evaluate the things in your life that are not serving you and that you are serving a little too much. Indicators that you may be serving something too much are restlessness, decline in happiness and enthusiasm towards that thing you love most, and you can even take a second to listen to the people closest to you because they tend to know, but most importantly, consult God.

The good thing about having great family members or friends is that they make great accountability partners, they tend to be able to see past all of the things that you've been blinded from, and they are not afraid to tell you when you're doing too much ! Get some of those good accountable people around you. People that can tell you when you're making a good, bad, or terrible decision.

I've come to learn that decisions truly help shape your life. So be mindful of everything you think and feel because ultimately that's how decisions are made. You ever see someone who a lot of people call crazy? It's normally because that person has made a slew of poor emotion-led decisions or the poor thoughtless and emotionless decisions. You see great decision-making is made by first analyzing exactly what the task at hand is, determining the main stakeholders (listening to how they feel) and/or who the decision will impact, and the big why!

"Why are you making the decision in the first place and how will it benefit you in the future?" By taking these steps it will be difficult for you to forget about yourself and others in your decision making.

Often, you'll see people leave out certain parts of this process which leads to destruction. For example, in this scenario a devoted wife constantly pleads for her husband to think about her more. Her husband feels that when he pays the bills, he is being thoughtful. However, she constantly tells him she just wants to spend some time together. The reason she still feels he is thoughtless is because he is not considering step 2, Determining the main stakeholders, and listening to how they feel!

With this model you can hardly ever go wrong with decision-making. Be it, for yourself or others. We're on a mission to keep as many of the good people around us as possible!

Speaking of good people around you... By this time, a couple months had passed and my mom and I made up. After the move out of my apartment, Jay and I broke up and I moved back in with my mom. After a long day of work, I came home and greeted my mother and aunt as usual. I turned the corner and went down the hall to my bedroom. This was the day that reality truly set in. It came out of nowhere after all this time. I was angry with Jay and myself. I went to my bedroom, closed the door softly, careful not to alert anyone else in the house that something was wrong with me this day, and sat on the carpet floor facing the window opposite of my bedroom door. This was done purposely just in case someone came in, they wouldn't be able to see what was really going on with me.

However, I knew it was only a matter of time before my mom came in. Before she did though, I did my best to have a silent cry to only myself and God. Tears rolled down my face and before I knew it, "*Knock, knock …. creeeeeek.*" As my room door opened, my mother slightly came in obnoxiously loud hurling jokes as only a New York mom can and trying to talk to me before realizing what I was doing on the other side of the bed. I did my best to answer her so that she would just go away. But when I opened my mouth, I gave myself away. Nothing could come out but a screeching earthshaking wail! My mom rushed over to me and sat on the floor next to me as she laid my head on her chest and rocked me back and forth as she use to do when I was a baby. She hugged me tight as I sobbed uncontrollably. She asked me what was wrong and all I could yell between cries was, "It's still not fair! I forgive him but this isn't fair! My life shouldn't be like this!" My mom continued to console me and assured me that, "He would get his one day." However, revenge wasn't what I wanted. I just really wanted him to understand the gravity of what was done and the hell I was going through. That moment made me realize that although this was my second chance at life and I knew good things would come out of starting over; sometimes you just need to cry. Let it out and move on. Allow yourself to feel all the emotions but don't dwell on them. So, I breathed in slowly and as air filled my lungs, my head started to rise. Then I exhaled and made the decision that this day would be the first day of the rest of my life.

The decision I made that day was a huge one that allowed me to really understand that every day is exactly what you make it and you can get through anything that you make up in your mind to do. It's not going to be easy but you're going to have to put in the work.

Chapter 6: Memories of the Past life

Next, I knew I had to get rid of all his clothing, jewelry, and items that he gave me. You see, not because I wasn't over him but because they just left a trail of the old life, pre-bankruptcy. I felt like I had been cleansed and given a second chance, so I didn't need any reminders of what once was, lingering around in my new life.

This process was so freeing for me. Of course, things were harder to get rid of than others, but emotional ties can tie you to the wrong thing. For the things that were harder to get rid of I put them in a separate pile. Now, let's be completely transparent, I did not have a "Waiting to Exhale" moment and throw all his things out in a ranging fit and light them on fire. Maybe about a month or two prior I would have though :). No, that there, was a process. For the things I absolutely couldn't part with I left them around for a while until I was ready, but I still held myself accountable. I did that by ensuring not everything went into this "sacred pile." But only, absolute special things. This part of the journey made me realize how important self-accountability is. I could've easily just kept everything. But, then what good would it do for me? It would be like cheating on your test by circling the same answers as your neighbor, only to find out they had a different version of the test than you. You put in a lot of work for absolutely nothing. After all you've been through in this life, the last person you need to cheat you is YOU. Don't knock value off the priceless commodity that is you. From here on, we're only adding value.

Can you believe even after all I went through, part of me wanted him back? I had to step back and really assess where those feelings were coming from. Were they coming from a place of love and wanting to work out my relationship? Or just from a place of codependency like in the past. It wasn't until later, after truly assessing my emotions, that I realized I didn't want him back, that I wanted that safe space back... no matter how toxic. During those times, you're going to have to truly access where your emotions are coming from. Remember, this will be an emotional time.

However, assessing those emotions will assist you in ensuring you're not acting out of anything but love. You see, most bad decisions derive from people feeling hurt, sadness, or anger which are all terrible emotions. Leading with anything but love (and not following the decision-making process from earlier) will have you in a constant cycle of doing the same things that you'd wish you hadn't.

So, what did I do to prevent this never-ending cycle? I faced reality.

I could only "show face" for so long until everyone could see that neither of us were actually happy. Not realizing this was the best thing for me though. Which brings me to my next point. Along with assessing your emotions, assess where you are in people's lives. At this life changing time, you do not need any distractions (aka people) that will bring anything less than positivity to your life. The word says you will know them by their fruit. In this case it meant I will know who is good and who isn't good in my life by what they bring to my life. For example, if you have a friend who has a problem for every solution you try to bring, chances are… it's time to distance yourself. Or, if you have a friend and/or family member who can't seem to be genuinely happy for you… chances are… It's time to distance yourself. In my situation, I had to stop lying to myself and recognize who I was to him in his eyes and I did this by assessing his actions. After my assessment, it was evident that I was disposable to him. Now, there is a disclaimer to utilizing this process. Only do these assessments when you are ready for the outcome. Unfortunately, at times they can be brutal. Let's face it everyone wants to feel important to someone, especially, the people that matter the most.

Now, don't get me wrong, facing reality is not about shutting people out of your life. That never ends well. Facing reality is about coming to grips on where you are in life and everything that you don't like that's going on, and making measurable steps to get to the end goal which is to have a healthy and enriching life in every aspect. That's Spiritually, Financially, Mentally, Emotionally, Physically, and in your relationships.

So, we already went through the first step of reality which is cutting out toxic people. The next step may hurt a little bit because it's going to cause you to be honest with yourself. You must cut out your bad and toxic habits. Yep! Hurts right? I know.... The best way I can say to ensure you are on the right path for this goal is keeping your commitments to yourself. For example, if you said you would go to the gym at 3PM. Be at the gym (actually working out, not in the parking lot. Been there! Done that.) by 3PM. Don't give yourself any reason not to. This also goes for your financial habits as well. Let me say that again, "Your financial habits." IF you know buying lunch everyday with your co-workers ends up with you having little to no money at the end of the month, then news flash - you need to stop buying the food! I bet your food tastes 1000 times better anyway. And, if you're a person who can't cook, there's always YouTube University.

So now, this leads me to my last point, your third step into reality is setting measurable goals with specified benchmarks. This was the part I kept messing up on. You see, I had the measurable goals part down. However, the specified benchmarks part was a consistent fail on my end. Specified benchmarks are in a nutshell a timeline that you can out to your goal.

For example, let's flashback to Jay and me for a moment.

Reality was closing in on us fast because my lease was going to be up. He wanted us to get another apartment together so badly, but I honestly wanted to get back into the will of God. Our plan was for him to move back in with his mom and for me to move back in with mine. I suffered so much criticism for this. People kept saying it was so backwards. (Again, watch your circle.) But I felt like backwards was me moving in with my boyfriend when he had not committed yet. It didn't matter though, because backwards was exactly what I needed. I wanted to rewind everything that took place within that year. He just wanted to keep going though.

Jay felt like if we moved out of our apartment then we'd break up. He was right. The Lord had already told me what to do and to stick with it. So, no matter how much I wanted to stay with him, I knew he wasn't the right one for me. I was told this during one of my many nights of sitting on the floor crying, staring out at the pool and moon from my bedroom window.

One of those nights I cried because I didn't want to let go but at the same time... I did. There's nothing like being in a situation where you're torn. For me, my most difficult situations, where I must make a decision, always happens when my heart and mind don't agree. I was stuck in this place.

So, this is a perfect example of poor decision making because I allowed my lease to be up before calling the relationship quits. I knew it wasn't the relationship I wanted to be in any longer, but I did not set a benchmark. I allowed outside forces to make the decision for me. In the new season, we are making our own intelligent, informed choices.

It's not going to be pretty, but it will be worth it.

Chapter 7: Breakthrough

A part of you has died. You're right. After going through bankruptcy whether it's your 1st,2nd, or 3rd + time. Understand that it's a closing of not just a Chapter 7 or 13 when you're discharged, but a closing on that chapter of your life. No longer will you be bound by what people say, society, or even what you have to say about yourself. Continue to think positively on everything you have done up until this point. How God brought you this far. There has never been a better time to reclaim your time, your life, and seize every good and perfect opportunity that God has for you.

This thing will be a breeze if you allow it. Take one step at a time and realize that this isn't a race to get back where you use to be, when your credit was "great" or when you had any "Credit card you wanted." This is another chance to take things slowly and realize where you messed up or made a bad critical decision so that you can build a strong financial foundation for the future.

During this process, allow all parts of you to heal. This is not just a physical thing and you should realize that. Starting over isn't always the easiest part of life but thank God that we're able to do it!

You will find yourself rejoicing before you know it. Live life! Be free! Live conscious daily! Be mindful that every small decision made impacts the decisions that follows. So, if you're thinking about going over 30% on your credit card for that new dress or any other unnecessary item... DON'T YOU DO IT!

Please know that in this season it's okay to be by yourself and concentrate on you. Don't allow others to guilt trip you into going out and spending more than you have. Don't allow family members or friends to demean you. Understand that you will have to go at your own pace. Did you know that this is one of the biggest waves of your life? Even in surfing, surfers understand that bigger waves are usually steeper. They say when riding a bigger wave, you shouldn't use a fat-nose longboard (typically used to make longer strides) and that you should use something smaller with a pointier nose. You see in this season you don't necessarily need to try to get to your destination so quickly but rather be equipped with the right tools and pointed focus. Yea, I know it's upsetting that you won't be able to do everything because now you have a smaller board and not enough room for it all. But sometimes, you have to get to where it's just you and God to get to the end goal. You don't have to have many possessions. In this case, it's setting ourselves up for financial freedom.

Surfers know when riding a big wave, the most important thing is paddling correctly, which is about timing and paddling extremely hard. The first thing is getting the board moving in the water as the wave approaches. You see, they don't just get in the water and attempt to go at the wave. No, so just Ride your wave at the pace God has you on and enjoy the journey.

With this rebuilding stage you are being restored from the inside out. Look at you shine! You are no longer bound by past decisions, bad choices, and/or self-doubt, but God has called you out of this as He called the people out of Egypt. God will restore, rebuild, and replenish. Please have faith in Him. I love you. God loves you.... YOU GOT THIS! NOW BREAKTHROUGH!

Tips that I used for getting out of debt

Hello again! I didn't think it would be right to leave you without some quick tips that I used to rebuild my credit quickly. Disclaimer: This is by no means any financial advice nor am I advising you to take these steps as I am not a professional financial advisor.

1. I applied for a secured card – This card allowed me to start seeing positive remarks and boosts in my credit within 1-3 months. It also helped me to gradually trust myself again with credit cards

2. I applied for a car loan – Keep in mind, most dealerships do have special programs for people who have just filed bankruptcy. In this part, don't get hung up on the negatives. Meaning, was my interest rate kind of high – Yes! However, refinancing within a year to a year and a half is always an option that's available.

3. After 6-8 months I applied for another line of credit through an online store. After paying that on time for 3-4 months and

not paying the minimum payment due, I watched my credit score, skyrocket.

4. Give yourself time. This process will not happen overnight and after reading this book, you'll find that it can be very emotional to go from Bankruptcy to Breakthrough. So, do not put extra pressure on yourself by rushing this process. Giving yourself time will allow you to learn new things about yourself and discover the new you. Also, it doesn't hurt that during this time some inquiries will fall off.

I love you and God loves you! Now, let's break through!

Acknowledgements

The completion of this book could not be done without the support and guidance of Candace Bazemore. Thank you for the countless hours of patience, time, and help. I will forever remember your role in getting my vision out to the world. I appreciate you more than you'll ever know.

To my friends and family (too many to name), thank you so much for your support and excitement for me!

To my Apostle and Pastor High, thank you so much for seeing the vision of this and helping light the fire for me to complete it. You all have been nothing but supportive in my journey and I couldn't thank you enough.

Lastly, to all the people I wish to touch with this book. I want to acknowledge you because this was all for you all. My prayer is that you are changed from the inside out.

www.ingramcontent.com/pod-product-compliance
Lightning Source LLC
Chambersburg PA
CBHW051358150726

48000CB00003B/1235